Adventures Of
TOY BOY
AND THE UNEXPECTED
EXPERIENCE

Book 3

Never
give up!

SMITH BARNER

ISBN-13: 978-1986087643
ISBN-10: 1986087646

CONTENTS

CHAPTER ONE

~The Beginning of Toy Boy's Gift~

Hi. My name is John Puram, but I go by the name Toy Boy. Not everyone knows that I go by this name, but I needed something fancy to be called, because I kind of believe that I am special. You probably want to know what is special about me, do you? Well you see, one night when I was sleeping, an angel appeared in front of me, and said that I was going to be able to start solving problems. Wow! I am only in the fourth grade, and I was wondering how little old me was going to be able to solve problems - and when!

I didn't know what to expect. But what do you know - my Supreme Man toy started talking! At first it was kind of scary. But I quickly got used to it. And then my Supreme Man toy came flying towards me. Could it be possible? I had never seen anything like it. One of my toys talking to me. It made me wonder why I did not scream out loud, so my mother could come and save me. Was I going crazy, or was this possible? Anyway, my Supreme Man toy introduced himself and we soon became friends. But this was only the beginning. Supreme Man told me that others would be helping me, and for a while nothing else happened, but then things started to crop up and I found I could do something about them. It's been a real adventure, with Supreme man; that time we solved the missing diamond at the museum was a great feeling. Then there was that time we stood up for the new kid, and the bully left him alone. I love solving different problems with my toys. I can't wait to solve more problems.

Then, one rainy night, my Molecule Woman came to me. I almost smashed her before I realized! I saw what looked like a bug running towards me. But before I could do anything, Supreme Man told me he had asked her to appear to me. What do you know, she grew bigger for me to see her!

That was how this whole incredible world started for me. My toys and I have had a lot of fun solving problems together. And now I wonder what's next, and whether another one of my toys is going to be joining us.

CHAPTER TWO

~Toy Boy's New Dream~

I knew I was dreaming. It had to be a dream, because I was riding a new BMX bike. And the thing about it was, I didn't remember having a new bike. My mother usually only buys me a gift for me on special occasions, and my birthday wasn't for a couple of months. But this bike was nice. Even the color was great. It was chrome and red, with pegs on the wheels. And on top of that, the spokes were Dayton's.

The dream was teasing me, because I couldn't believe I was riding a bike like this. My mother is taking care of me by herself, and she probably couldn't afford a bike like this. Wow, I really shouldn't be disappointed while I'm asleep, but I couldn't help it. It almost seemed like a nightmare, because I really would like to own a bike like this.

Maybe this dream was about the future, or maybe it was just a dream, and I would only be able to ride it when I was asleep. Could I really get a bike like this? How? A dream I had before really delivered a miracle to my life. So was I still going to receive new miracles? I needed to wake up. Ringggggggggggggggggg, my alarm clock went.

CHAPTER THREE

~The Attempt at Toy Boy's New Toy Appearance~

"Good morning, Toy Boy," said Supreme Man excitedly. "I have a new surprise for you."

"Which one of my toys is going to help us this time?" I asked.

"I really do not know," he said. "I never know until moments before they are ready to appear."

"That doesn't seem surprising," I said.

"You should have more faith than that," said Molecule Woman.

"This is puzzling," said Supreme Man. "I am not getting a response. Something is not right;

I should have had a response by now."

"This isn't supposed to happen," said Molecule Woman. "I wonder what is going wrong?"

"How do you feel, Toy Boy?" asked Supreme Man. "Is something bothering you?"

"No," I said. "I'm okay, I guess."

"It is important that nothing is wrong with you," said Supreme Man. "Otherwise it affects the process, and your new toy will not come alive for you. Well, let's try again. But this time, try to think of something positive, so things can go right for you."

"Okay," I said, "but I don't think anything is wrong with me."

"Well, there does still seem to be something wrong," Supreme Man replied. "I'm not getting any response."

"Wow," I said. "Things are starting to be unbelievable now." I was starting to feel quite anxious.

"Well it all depends on how much you believe, Toy Boy," said Molecule Woman. "If you only believe anything is possible, then things will work out for the best."

"Can you try it again?" I asked sadly. "Or maybe no more toys will come to life for me? It's already a miracle that you guys are with me."

"Miracles happen all the time, Toy Boy,"

Supreme Man said confidently. "God really cares, and until you realize that anything is possible, then things are not going to work out the way they should."

CHAPTER FOUR

~Toy Boy Is Disappointed~

"I don't understand this at all," I said, disappointed. "I was really happy about having my toys helping me, and now it's all going wrong. I should have known everything wouldn't go right for me. Maybe God doesn't see me as a good person any more. Or maybe this is nothing but a terrible dream. Life was just getting interesting. Why doesn't God let me know more? What did I do wrong? Was it because of what we did to Tony for trying to bully Timothy? Maybe I shouldn't have made Tony look like he was going crazy? Is God mad at me or something? I need to solve this issue. I enjoy you guys helping solve these problems. So what do I need to do to get more toys to come alive and help me?"

"It has to come with from something within you," said Molecule Woman.

"OK, so what is the difference between now and when both of you came alive?" I asked. "I really don't see a difference."

"John! Time to get ready for school!" yelled my mother from downstairs.

"I am not going to school today, because I am starting not to feel so good," I told Supreme Man and Molecule Woman.

"I don't feel good today, Mom." I yelled back to her.

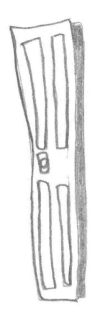

"Come down here," shouted my mother. "Let me check and see if you have a fever."

I came downstairs slowly, with my head down and a sad face. I walked up to my mom.

"You don't have a high temperature," she said, staring intently at me. "It's not like you to want to miss school. Is it your belly?"

"I just don't feel myself, Mom."

"Well, okay, but you need to put something in your stomach."

"I only want a little cereal," I told her. "I'm not very hungry."

"Okay, well try to get some rest," she said.

CHAPTER FIVE

~Toy Boy Gets Scared~

"Today was a boring, gloomy day," I said to Supreme Man. "But I didn't want to go to school. Matter of fact, I really don't feel like doing anything."

"You need to find some way to get happy again," suggested Supreme Man.

That night, as I got into bed, I saw something moving in my closet.

"Did either of you see that?" I asked, frightened. "There's something moving in my closet. I thought you guys could interpret the future."

"The real power comes from within you,"

said Molecule Woman. "Right now, you're not quite yourself, and that's preventing us from having a good connection with you. I think you have got spoiled by the fact you have toys that come alive."

"That's right – but just relax, and everything you want might happen when you want it to happen," said Supreme Man. "You must know that we will not let anything happen to you. And that is very important for you to understand."

"I'm trying to deal with everything," I told him, "but not being able to witness another miracle is kind of upsetting."

"But we are here to help you," said Molecule Woman. "That's part of our responsibility."

"But how am I going to deal with things?" I asked. And why did I have a dream about a bike?

"Well," said Supreme Man, "try to remember

how you felt when we first appeared to you. It was all new then, that we came to you, but you dealt with it anyway."

"Wow," I said. "I can see it's going to be a long night. Just thinking about something moving in my closet gives me the creeps."

"This is something you have to deal with yourself," replied Supreme Man, "but I can tell you it is probably a test of your willpower."

"Huh. How can I believe something is not going to harm me if I don't know what to expect to happen next? How will I ever get any rest? Do you think one of you could read me a bedtime story?"

"Neither one of us is equipped with that gift," said Molecule Woman, "But I am sure you will be sent one who can."

CHAPTER SIX

~Supreme Man and Molecule Woman Help with Toy Boy's Faith~

"Good Morning, Toy Boy," said Supreme Man.

"Is it Saturday already?" I asked. "It's been a long night. I was glad I had you guys to talk to. I didn't think I was ever going to get to sleep. I wonder what today will be like."

"You've got to keep hope alive," said Molecule Woman. "I mean, you have to believe that everything is going to work out for the best."

"See," added Supreme Man, "there is one thing you can always do to help your situation, and that is to pray."

"So you're telling me," I said, "that all I have to do is pray and everything will be okay? That won't be hard. As a matter of fact, that is a good deal. I remember when my mother used to pray for me. I guess it's time for me to pray for myself. So what should I pray for?"

"How about praying to God to restore your faith? Molecule Woman suggested. "To us, that seems to be the only thing you are lacking."

"I think you're right," I said. "I don't feel like myself just now. Supreme Man, I believe I will go to church tomorrow. I haven't been in a while, and maybe I need a little push."

"John," called my mother from downstairs. "Come down and eat your breakfast."

"Mom," I said, a few minutes later, "I've been thinking. What would you say if I asked you to go to church tomorrow?"

"Sure, I see you're growing up," she said, surprising me. I hurried up and ate my breakfast, then ran upstairs to spend time with my toys.

"I'm sure you are going to be okay, Toy Boy. Going to church is going to be a big turnaround for you," Molecule Woman stated with certainty.

"My mother was happy with the idea," I said. "And that makes me feel better about myself."

"Just relax and don't worry, because you will soon see that you are taking a big step in life," said Supreme Man.

CHAPTER SEVEN

~Toy Boy's Reality Check~

The next morning, my mother and I went to church. The preacher at the church really got through to me. He was talking about faith. He said everybody should believe that everything is going to be alright, even if you don't know what's going to happen next. I think the pastor's message was something I really needed to hear. It changed the way I saw the world. I truly think the Lord was with me, and that He had never left me. I had been having negative thoughts, but now I found myself thinking positive.

When I made it home, I ran to my room to

tell my toys the good news.

"I feel wonderful," I told them. "I'm looking at the world differently now."

"That is good, Toy Boy," Molecule Woman replied. "I can sense that you have had a good look at your life."

"You are surely right," I said enthusiastically. "I believe everything is going to be alright. My mind is more focused, and my thoughts are on good things. I now keep hope alive, and I have faith. And, you know, life is enjoyable again. This day has been a good experience for me."

"That is fantastic," said Supreme Man, "and now I see a brighter future for you."

CHAPTER EIGHT

~Another Toy Comes to Life~

"Good morning, Toy Boy," Supreme Man said as I awoke. "Guess what I have in store for you."

"What is it?" I asked.

"Your Super Bear has come to life to help us solve more mysteries," he said happily.

"That's wonderful," I said. "So a new miracle has happened! I love it!"

"Hi, Toy Boy," said Super Bear. "Today I am full of joy!"

"So what took you so long to appear?" I asked him.

"Well, I needed you to have faith for me to come alive for you," he replied. "You see, my gift is that I can change the outcomes of situations. Like on days when you are not feeling happy, one touch from me and you will start to be happy again. But when Molecule Woman sees that things might end up going wrong, then I could make them turn out well. So can you see why it took a lot of faith for me to come to life?"

"I surely do," I told him. "The gift you have could not afford to be in the wrong hands."

"I also have good news for you. Your father will be sending you a new BMX bike pretty soon," Molecule Woman said.

"But thanks to your faith and my gift," added Super Bear, "it will be here by the time you get home from school."

"Well, I'm going to get ready for school," I told my toys. "This weekend been very special for me. I've really learned a lot from it."

"I would be glad to go to school with you if you want me to," said Super Bear.

"That would be fantastic," I replied. "As a matter of fact, I'd love to have all three of you with me."

CHAPTER NINE

~Having Faith~

"Hi, Dan," I said to my best friend. "How was your weekend?"

"It was great!" he said. "How was your weekend, and why weren't you in school Friday?"

"Well I wasn't feeling the best, but as the weekend came to an end, I started believing that things weren't as bad as they seemed." Then I told him that I had been to church, and had learned about faith.

"What did you learn?" he asked. "And who is your new toy?"

"This is Super Bear," I told him. "And I

learned that you're supposed to believe that everything is going to be alright, even if you don't know what's going to happen next."

When I walked into the class, and Tony saw me with my toys, he screamed out, "There goes Toy Boy!" The rest of the class laughed. But it didn't bother me, because that was the name I wanted to be called. Everything was coming true, as if all these things I was experiencing were supposed to happen.

At the end of the day, the bell rung for dismissal.

"I am starting to feel special," I told my toys.

"You are special," Super Bear told me. "And don't think anything different."

"You can believe no one is going to be able to change my mind," I replied. We all laughed.

CHAPTER TEN

~ Toy Boy's New Bike Arrives~

When I got home, my mother had the bike waiting for me. "John, your father has sent you a bike, she told me. "He said he wanted it to be a surprise."

"Wow," I said excitedly. "I'm so happy! And from now on I'm going to try to have a positive attitude about everything."

ABOUT THE AUTHOR

Hi, I'm Smith Barner a children's author who likes basketball, strawberry banana smoothies and spending time with my family. I served in the Marines Corp and I'm now a disabled veteran, who writes books. One of my favorite things to do is operating a business. I have a few books currently available for purchase. Which are, Adventures of Toy Boy and the lost Diamond and Adventures of Toy Boy and the New Kid in School.

BACKLIST

Adventures of Toy Boy and the lost Diamond BK1

Adventures of Toy Boy and the New Kid in School BK2

Adventures of Toy Boy and the Unexpected Experience

BK3

More Books Coming Soon!

THANK YOU

I would like to thank my Father in heaven for giving me the talent to write children books. I also would like to thank my wonderful wife for being such a huge encouragement to me. She's a huge help and I couldn't have done this without her. To my wonderful daughter, she's my joy and one of the reasons I write these books! Thank you to my cover designer for making my books look amazing, Patti Roberts. Thank you, Tabitha O. Smith for editing my book, you do wonders. I also would like to thank my illustrator. And thank you to all that read this book, I hope you enjoy your children reading this book or if you are reading to them!

Smith M Barner

CONTACT THE AUTHOR

I love to hear from readers and if you would like to contact, follow or have questions these links will lead you to me!

FB - https://www.facebook.com/Smitty-Barner-Childrens-Author-420187958319426/

FB personal page - https://www.facebook.com/profile.php?id=100015668828425

Website – www.barnervillage.com

Instagram - https://www.instagram.com/smittybarner/

Email – smittychildrensbook@gmail.com

If you have enjoyed this book, please consider leaving a short review for me and help me spread the word on social media. With appreciation, Smith Barner.

Made in the USA
Monee, IL
18 May 2021